THE
ONE
BAD
THING
ABOUT
BIRTHDAYS
by David Collins
illustrated by David Wiesner

It's David's birthday, and all his friends are gathered round the huge cake. But before he can blow out the candles, he has to make a wish, and *that's* the problem with birthdays—what to choose? A bubble gum prescription from the dentist? Permission to watch scary movies? A ton of mail that's all for him? Finally, he realizes what the one wish should be....

David Wiesner's spirited drawings capture David's imaginings and his guests' growing impatience, in this funny look at familiar childhood wishes.

About the Book

David loves birthdays! He especially
loves making a birthday wish as he blows out
the candles on his cake. But what should he
wish for? Endless cookies baked by Grandma?
Fishing alone with Grandpa? Being allowed
to stay up late to watch a monster movie
on television? David's dilemma is a familiar
one, and everybody will applaud the wish
he finally chooses.

A LET ME READ BOOK

DAVID R. COLLINS

The One Bad Thing About Birthdays

ILLUSTRATED BY DAVID WIESNER

HARCOURT BRACE JOVANOVICH   NEW YORK AND LONDON

To *my* mother, who made *my* birthday possible

Printed in the United States of America

LIBRARY OF CONGRESS CATALOGING IN PUBLICATION DATA
Collins, David R
The one bad thing about birthdays.
(A Let me read book)
SUMMARY: A boy tries to decide what to wish for on
his birthday.
[1. Birthdays—Fiction.   2. Wishes—Fiction]
I. Wiesner, David.   II. Title.
PZ7.C6955On   [E]   80-23104
ISBN 0-15-258288-6   ISBN 0-15-258289-4 pbk.

B C D E   FIRST EDITION   B C D E   (PBK)

I like birthdays.
Mom always puts lots of frosting
on *my* birthday cake.

Everybody sings "Happy Birthday."
Then I blow out the candles
and make a wish. That's the
one bad thing about birthdays.
I get to make only one wish.

I wish I could make more wishes
on my birthday.

I wish my dad would say,
"David, your trike is too little.
It's time you had a bike."

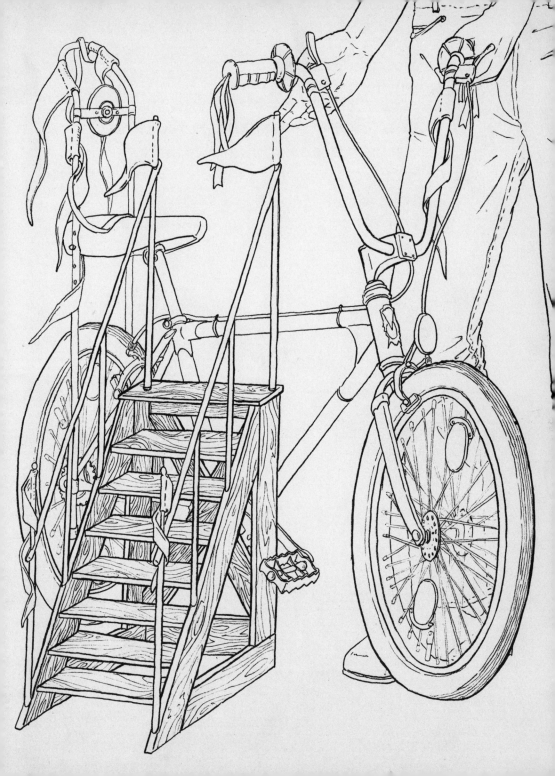

I wish my mom would say,
"Sure you can watch
this movie, David. It's got
lots of monsters in it."

I wish my big brother would say,
"Come on along with us, David.
All my friends think you're great."

I wish my big sister would say,
"Of course, you may use the bathroom,
David. I'll get right out."

And that Aunt Carol would say,
"You certainly have grown, David.
And I'm not going to pinch your cheek
this time."

I wish Grandpa would say,
"Let's go fishing, David. Just you and me."

And that Grandma would say,
"Have another cookie, David.
You've had only six."

I wish our neighbor Miss Burnside would say,
"You can cut across my yard anytime, David.
I won't tell your mother."

And that Mr. Clark down the block would say,
"Take some apples, David. My tree
always has too many."

I wish the barber would say,
"You don't need a haircut, David.
But here's a sucker anyway."

I wish my dentist would say,
"You'll have to chew more bubble gum,
David. It's good for you."

And that our postman would say,
"All the mail's for you today, David."

And that the paper boy would say,
"Look, David! Your picture's
on the front page!"

I wish my teacher would say,
"Your writing is fine, David.
It's not scribbly any more."

And, oh, how I wish big Josh Harvey at school would say, "David's going to be on *my* team."

Birthdays are great.
But I wish I didn't have
to wait a whole year to
make another birthday wish.